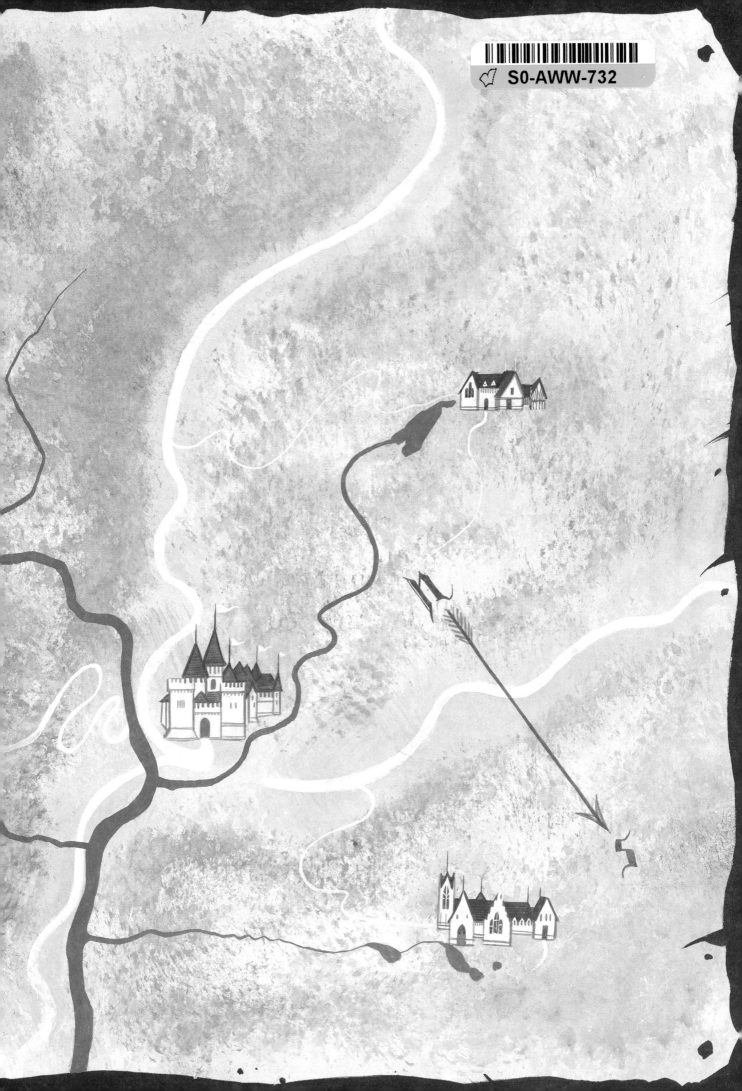

Printed and bound in Malaysia

ISBN 0-517-06523-1

87654321

ROBIN HOOD

Re-told by Michael Bishop
Illustrated by Gerry Embleton

DERRYDALE BOOKS
New York

When Richard I—Richard the Lion
Heart—was King of England, there
grew up on the edge of the Forest of
Sherwood near Nottingham a youth
called Robin Hood. He was the son of
an honest yeoman who tilled the soil to
keep his family in as much comfort as
was possible in those days.

Young Robin learned the ways of the
forest, often in the company of his
cousin, Tim, and his lifelong
sweetheart, Marian. They led a free
and happy life and went in for all sorts
of games and sports. Robin was good at
them all, but there was one at which
none could beat him.

This was archery—shooting arrows
from the traditional longbow. He could
score a bulls-eye at two hundred paces
and then split the first arrow in two
with his next shot.

When he was young, archery was nothing but a sport to be practiced with his friends. But as he grew to be a young man Robin took his bow and a quiver full of arrows whenever he went far from home, for he lived in dangerous times.

One day he went to the annual fair in Nottingham town together with Tim and Marian. They were wandering happily past the many stalls of merchants noisily selling their wares when they were accosted by four youths of the town making fun of their country clothes.

"Take no notice," said Robin, taking Marian's arm.

"Aye, that's a pretty wench!" called out one of the townies with a threatening gesture. "Maybe she'd like to be with us rather than a couple of country bumpkins!"

That did it.

In a flash Robin had punched him once in the midriff and once on the jaw. He fell back onto his companions. They let him fall and went for Robin with their cudgels. But Tim was there first, fending off their blows with his staff while Robin used his fists to good effect. In no time a full-scale fight had started with country folk fighting for Robin and Tim and townsmen backing the youths.

As soon as they could Robin and Tim escaped from the uproarious melee of flying fists and swinging cudgels to protect Marian who was anxiously watching from the edge of the crowd. "Let's get out of here," said Robin. But at that moment a detachment of guards from the castle came onto the scene, alerted by the noise.

"There go the varmints who started it all!" shouted one of the townsmen.

Two of the guards turned towards Robin and his friends.

"Quick—up this alleyway!" urged Robin.

The three friends dodged up between two houses, but the guards had spotted them. One of them let off a bolt from his crossbow. It missed Marian's head by a hairsbreadth and buried itself in the side of one of the houses. "So that's your game, is it?" Robin was furious and fitted an arrow to his bow. He barely had time to take aim as the second guard was now racing into the alley brandishing a pike with a glint of steel at the tip. Robin let go the arrow—it hit the fellow full in the chest and bowled him over backwards.

"Oh, Robin! You've killed him," cried Marian. "Better him than you, Marian," answered Robin. "Come on!"

And the three of them fled into the maze of little streets and alleyways where the poor people of the town lived.

News that one of his guards had been killed reached the Sheriff of Nottingham very quickly. He promptly mustered as many men as he could. "Catch the villain!" he roared. "By thunder, he'll pay dearly for this."

His men were spurred on by the knowledge that the sheriff put a price on the head of every outlaw. "Ten pieces of silver to the first to bring him in, dead or alive!" he cried.

But search as they might they never found any trace of Robin or his companions. The poor people of Nottingham had been for too long oppressed by their sheriff and his guards and were only too happy to help anybody trying to escape from them.

So the three of them found themselves on the edge of Sherwood Forest as dusk was falling. "Tim—you get Marian back home," said Robin. "You'll be safe now—it's me they're after. I will have to disappear for a while."

"I'll see that she's unharmed," said Tim. "Good luck, Robin!"

"Oh, Robin, where shall we see you again?" cried Marian. "Why—under the Greenwood tree," grinned Robin, and he strode off into the darkening forest.

Robin Hood slept rough that first night hidden in some bushes, but by dawn next day he was heading deeper and deeper into the forest. He knew that there was a band of outlaws hidden well away from all the known tracks, and he had a shrewd idea where to find them.

The sun had risen and was twinkling through the branches when suddenly an arrow twanged into a tree alongside him. Robin stopped dead.

"Who goes?" came a voice from ahead.

"I am known as Robin Hood."

"State your business, Master Robin."

"I am outlawed by the Sheriff of Nottingham. I seek the company of those in like circumstances," said Robin.

There was a pause and a whispered consultation.

"Come forward," said the voice. "Slowly—and no treachery!"

Robin pushed ahead through the thick undergrowth. Suddenly he was in a magnificent clearing in the forest, dominated by a mighty oak tree and a huge outcrop of rock, on which knelt a lone archer aiming an arrow straight at Robin.

Three men confronted him as he emerged from the bushes. "Aye," said one, "that's Robin Hood. Welcome to the Greenwood, Robin."

"Why, it's Much—Much the Miller's son," smiled Robin. "Methought I'd be among friends. Now tell yon bowman to put away his arrow!"

Robin looked around him and what he saw gave him much pleasure. A score of men were in the glade engaged in a variety of activities. One of them picked up a bow and shot an arrow at a target some hundred yards away. His arrow hit the bullseye with a thump.

"There, Master Robin Hood," he grinned. "Let's see you better that!"

Robin notched an arrow to his bow, took careful aim, and shot. His arrow hit the first one where it had entered the target and knocked it to the ground.

"Next time," said Robin, "give me something more difficult to do!"

And so Robin Hood joined the band of outlaws in Sherwood Forest.

Because of his skill with the longbow, he soon won their full respect and became their leader.

He began to organise them and to impose a certain discipline so that, as time went by, they became a force to be reckoned with in the forest. And he dressed them all in Lincoln green the better to blend in with the background. (All, that is, except one called Will Scarlett who was allowed to wear the scarlet hose that his family tradition decreed.)

Robin trained his men in archery, in swordsmanship, in combat with staves; he taught them to use the horn as a means of signalling and of rallying men from all parts of the forest; they went hunting deer together; and they spent hours perfecting their forest crafts.

It was a time of considerable strife in England. King Richard was out of the country much of the time fighting the Crusades. He left the government in the hands of his son, Prince John, who was weak and allowed too much power for rich men like the Sheriff of Nottingham.

Robin Hood managed to instil into his men a supreme loyalty to himself and to the King, and each one pledged his support for the poor and oppressed.

"We take from the rich and we give to the poor." Such was the avowed policy of Robin Hood and his band of outlaws.

Robin was out one day exploring new paths and routes through the forest. He came to a wide stream, swollen by recent rains, across which a tree trunk had fallen forming a bridge.

He approached it carefully—and suddenly became aware of a man on the other side, leaning on a staff as if guarding the bridge.

"That's a hefty fellow," Robin said to himself as he began to cross. "Out of the way, little one!" he called out loudly.

The man stepped onto the tree trunk, raising his staff. "Come on past," he said, "if you dare!"

"So that's the way of it, eh!" cried Robin, and aimed a swipe at him with his staff.

The big man blocked the blow with his own cudgel and, swift as lightning, swung it round in a line with Robin's head. Robin ducked and backed away. The big man nearly lost his balance, but managed to stay on the tree trunk.

The two men glared at each other, staffs at the ready.
"I'm going to cross this stream," said Robin.
"Not this way you're not," growled the other.

Robin jabbed at him with his staff. The big man
brushed the blow aside and went to poke Robin in
the stomach. But Robin was quicker and brought
his staff down on the other's head with a mighty
crack. The big man hardly blinked.

"So we're playing games now, are we?" he said
with a fiendish grin. And he brought his cudgel
round in a massive blow which caught Robin
square on the shoulder.

"That'll teach you to take on your betters," he grunted as Robin plunged headfirst into the stream. He came to the surface to see the big man grinning down at him. Robin stood up in the water.

"All right," he said. "You want to play games!" And he suddenly grabbed his opponent's foot and brought him tumbling down into the stream with him.

In and out of the water they fought for five minutes, ten minutes, quarter of an hour. Then Robin sent the big man reeling with a punch to the chin.

"Have you had enough yet?" he asked.

"I can go on like this all day," came the reply, and Robin just dodged a mighty blow to his head.

"Hold it," cried Robin. "Who are you and what are you doing in the forest?"

"They call me John and I've come to Sherwood to join a band of ruffians led by Robin Hood!"

"Little John," laughed Robin, "welcome to the Greenwood."

"And who might you be?" the other man asked, puzzled.

"Why, they call me Robin Hood!"

"Well, I'll be . . . !" roared Little John, holding out his hand. As they shook hands their laughter filled the forest with joyous sound.

It was in like manner that Robin Hood recruited many a brave and courageous fighter to his band of outlaws, testing them first in some form of combat.

Little John, sure enough, soon became second-in-command to Robin and remained his faithful friend and follower to the end.

But one of the strangest recruits to join the outlaws was found by Robin wandering in the forest. He was a fat friar in monkish robes pacing slowly through the trees, telling his beads and muttering strange incantations.

"Hail, there, Father," Robin greeted him. "What ails thee?"

"My son," he replied, "I was just contemplating the wickedness of this world."

"It seems to me," said Robin, "that some particular wickedness is taxing you at this moment."

"You are right, my son," said the friar. "I was lately one of the brothers in the Abbey of Pinkshill. I fear that our Lord Abbott was not a man of God—a very wicked man indeed—as I discovered to my cost."

"You've left Pinkshill then?" asked Robin.

"Two days ago. I've not slept since, nor washed, and my belly is sore with hunger."

"Well, now," said Robin, "if you have strength enough in that broad back of yours to carry me across yon stream, I could guide you to a feast fit for a—well, a friar."

"A pleasure, my son," smiled Friar Tuck as he waded through the water.

It was a very happy and contented Friar Tuck who wiped his lips with satisfaction as he threw away the last bone from the ribs of venison on which he had fed. Several of the men who had been watching him gazed in awe at his gargantuan appetite.

"That was a tasty little meal," he murmured appreciatively. "I should be well content to join this happy band."

"Ah!" said Robin Hood. "First you must prove yourself, Father. Despite your cloth, are you willing to fight?"

The Friar looked surprised but said nothing.

"Have you ever had to defend yourself?" asked Robin.

"Once or twice," nodded Friar Tuck gravely.

At a signal from Robin, two of his men attacked the stout friar with cudgels. Despite his size and the enormous meal he had just eaten, he was on his feet in a flash fending off their blows with ease.

Then, all of a sudden, he grabbed the two of them in his great arms and banged their heads together soundly. They both staggered away.

"Any more?" asked the Friar looking around.

"Methinks you've proved yourself," laughed Robin.

"Then, my son, it's now your turn." And in the blink of an eye he had leapt onto Robin's back. "If there's strength enough in that broad back of yours, you may carry me across yon pool," he said.

Robin staggered under the weight but managed to reach the pool—and tossed the Friar headfirst into the water!

As he sat himself up, dripping and spitting water, Robin said to him: "You said you hadn't washed, Father!"

From that day, Friar Tuck looked after the spiritual needs of the outlaws.

As on many another morning in the forest, two men armed with longbows lay hidden in the undergrowth close to one of the rough roads through the trees. One was Little John, the other was known as Merry Andrew.

After many hours of watching and listening, they heard the clip-clop of horse's hooves coming slowly closer. A figure on horseback appeared round a bend.

"He has a noble air," murmured Merry Andrew.

"Aye," replied Little John, "there's a tidy sum for our coffers there." He stood up, notching an arrow in his bow, and planted himself in the middle of the road in front of the horseman.

"What do you want with me?" demanded the bearded rider. "If it's money you're seeking, I have but ten shillings."

"Ho-ho!" laughed Little John, "we'll see about that. True—you have a hungry look about you. Would you care to have a fine dinner as a guest of Robin Hood?"

"Have I any choice?"

"I think not," agreed Little John. "Come now, Merry Andrew and I will guide you."

Merry Andrew stepped from the bushes and took the horse by the bridle.

"Welcome to the Greenwood, Sir Knight," Robin greeted his guest. "I trust that you can pay handsomely for your dinner."

"Robin," grinned Little John, "he says he has but ten shillings."

"Tis true, I swear," said the horseman dismounting. "You may search me and my bags."

Robin nodded to Little John, who went through the man's belongings with growing disbelief. He found only a few silver pieces.

"Ten shillings it is, Robin."

Robin turned to his guest. "How happens it that a man so obviously of noble birth travels abroad with so little to pay his way?"

"Tis a long, sad story," was the reply, "but if yon villain's promise of a dinner be true, I'll tell you while we sup."

"To the table, then," commanded Robin.

So, to the accompaniment of jugs of good wine and great dishes of venison, wild duck and guinea-fowl, the poor knight's story was told.

His name was Gilbert and he had lived in a modest castle near the Abbey of Pinkshill. One day he had taken part in a jousting tournament and had, most unfortunately, killed his opponent. Therefore he had had to pay a forfeit of 400 sovereigns, a vast sum in those days.

Not having sufficient funds to pay, he had been forced to borrow from the Abbott of Pinkshill and, in return, to give his castle and his lands in pledge.

"If the full sum is not paid by tomorrow, I shall lose everything I possess," he concluded sadly.

"Little John," said Robin, "think you that we could find some golden sovereigns in our treasury?"

"But Master Robin!" exclaimed Gilbert, "I could not possibly accept . . . !"

"Never fear, Sir Gilbert," smiled Robin, "if we can give you enough to pay off your debt to the Abbott, we have ways of getting it back again." And he winked at Friar Tuck.

Little John returned with leather bags full of coins. "Four hundred golden guineas," he announced.

"Robin, I . . . I cannot thank you enough," stammered the poor knight.

"Begone, Sir Gilbert," ordered Robin. "Go pay your dues to the Abbott."

The knight put the gold bags into his saddlebags, mounted his horse, and with a farewell salute to Robin and his men, he rode off.

Next morning, the Abbott of Pinkshill was at work on his accounts. He was gleefully anticipating that today was the day when that stupid Sir Gilbert's castle and lands would become his and add to his already considerable riches, when his steward announced the arrival of the knight.

"Welcome, Sir Gilbert," he said with a sneer. "I am assured that you have not acquired sufficient money to redeem your debt."

Gilbert appeared to be querulous. "My Lord Abbott," he pleaded, "Surely you can find it in your heart to give me a few more weeks . . ."

"Not a day more," pronounced the Abbott.

"Have you no mercy for me in my misfortune?"

"None, my dear Sir Gilbert," retorted the Abbott. "You have brought misfortune on yourself. The castle and your lands are MINE!"

"NEVER!" roared Sir Gilbert, producing his bags of gold. He flung them at the Abbott's feet. "There are your four hundred guineas," he said, scornfully. "The castle is mine!"

With that, he turned his back on the Abbott and strode out of the room. He mounted his horse which he had tethered at the gates of the Abbey.

And he galloped back to his castle.

A few days later, Robin Hood and Little John were able to intercept the Abbott on his way through the forest to pay his dues to the Sheriff of Nottingham.

The frightened Abbott was led to the outlaws' hideout, where a splendid meal had been prepared. He was seated between Robin and Little John who both plied him with food and wine until he protested that he could eat no more.

"May I go now?" he asked plaintively.

"Of course," said Robin. "When you've paid the bill."

"The . . . the bill?" stammered the Abbott.

"Just four hundred guineas," smiled Little John.

"B—b—b—but . . . !"

"Search his bags, Little John."

"It's all here, Robin," said Little John a few minutes later. "We've got our own back," he added as they watched a disconsolate Abbott riding off into the trees.

One day, Robin thought of a cunning scheme to help the poor people of Nottingham. All the meat sold in the town was very heavily taxed by the Sheriff making it impossible for many of the people to buy sufficient for their family needs.

So he arranged to set up a stall in the town where, disguised as a butcher, he gave away joints of venison. Many were the women of the town who blessed him for providing something so badly needed.

The news soon came to the ears of the Sheriff. He decided to find out how somebody could set up such a business which deprived him of his taxes.

He approached the man, who had become known as "The Mad Butcher", as he was packing up his stall.

"Tell me, my man," he commanded, "where is it you obtain your meat?"

"My Lord," answered Robin, "I will willingly take you to see the herds from which this meat is taken. But your Lordship must come alone."

"Why so?" asked the Sheriff.

"Your Lordship would not wish to share his profit with any others," said Robin with a knowing wink.

A little later, Robin Hood driving a meat cart, followed by the Sheriff on horseback, entered Sherwood. They made their way along little-known paths to a small clearing deep in the heart of the forest.

There before them were stags and does, peacefully grazing.

"These, my Lord Sheriff, are my herds," said Robin grandly.

"B—but," spluttered the Sheriff, "those are royal deer! Made into my care by the King's own bailiff! I will summon my guard to arrest you!"

"Not so, my Lord," grinned Robin. And producing his horn, he blew a ringing blast. In seconds, a score of archers all dressed in Lincoln green appeared from the trees on every side of the clearing. Each had an arrow aimed at the Sheriff.

"Have no fear, my Lord Sheriff," said Robin. "Tis only an invitation to dine with us."

"I'll not eat with outlaws!"

"One word from me," warned Robin, "and my archers loose their arrows!"

"I'll dine with you," said the Sheriff hastily.

Right royally they feasted him with great joints of venison and when he said he could eat no more they aimed their arrows at him—and he ate some more.

At last Robin said, "As you well know, my Lord Sheriff, meat is highly taxed in these parts. We must charge you fifty guineas for such a fulsome banquet."

The Sheriff protested, but when he saw the archers raise their long bows once more, he paid up.

"Fetch his horse, Little John, We'll send him on his way."

Little John had a mischievous grin on his face. "I'll warrant this steed knows his way back to Nottingham. What if we were to tie his Lordship to the saddle, facing backwards—so that we can all wave goodbye to him?"

"I'll have my revenge on you, Robin Hood!" swore the Sheriff through clenched teeth as he was packed off home—back to front.

This is the story of how Robin Hood paid good money to become a hangman! Little John and Will Scarlett were carrying out one of their normal patrols in the forest when they unexpectedly walked into a contingent of the Sheriff's guards.

Despite a furious fight, Little John was captured—but he held off the soldiers long enough to enable Will to get away.

As soon as he heard the news, Robin Hood set off for Nottingham with a score of his men, all in disguise. By the time they got there, a scaffold had already been erected in one of the main squares and a public execution of the outlaw had been announced for the following morning.

Robin found the hangman who had been charged with the execution and bribed him to change places. Robin put on the hangman's clothes and allowed him to leave the city a considerably richer man.

Next morning, all was prepared. A crowd of townspeople had gathered in the square; the noose hung from the wooden scaffold; the 'hangman' was ready.

There was a sudden hush in the crowd. The sound of marching feet was heard.

Six guards appeared. Little John was in their midst, head erect, towering above them.

They approached the scaffold and halted at a harsh command.

There was scarcely a murmur from the crowd but many of the women wept. They were now waiting for the Sheriff to arrive to give the order for the execution.

But, suddenly, the 'hangman' produced a horn and blew a resounding clarion call.

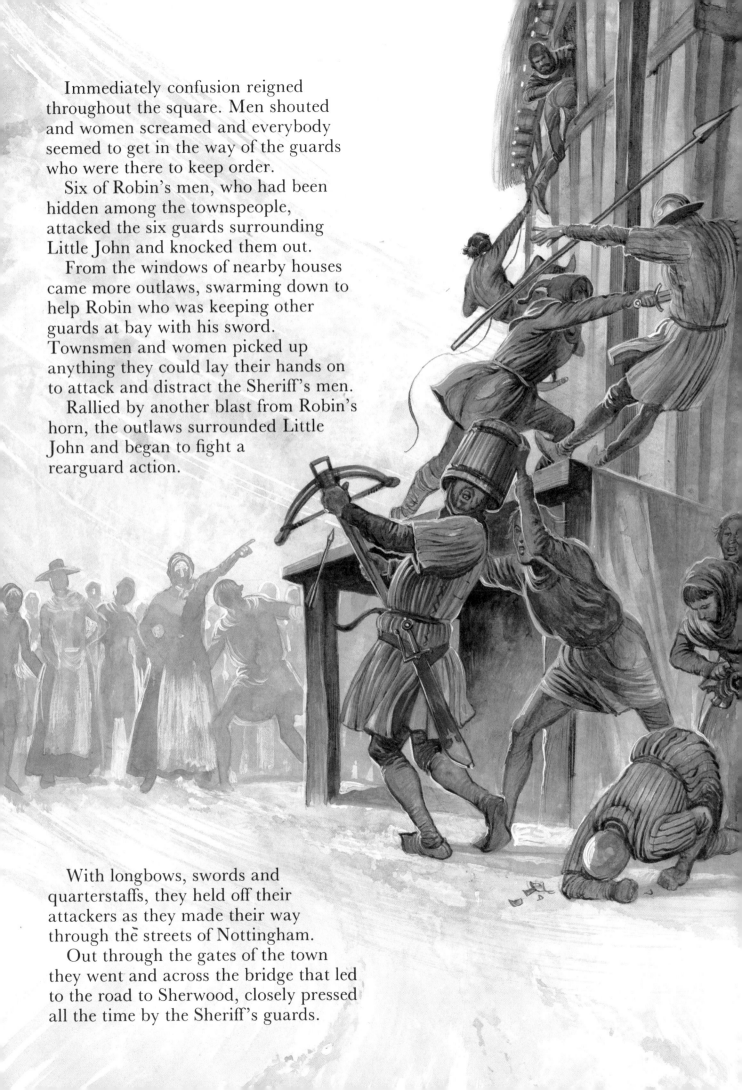

Immediately confusion reigned throughout the square. Men shouted and women screamed and everybody seemed to get in the way of the guards who were there to keep order.

Six of Robin's men, who had been hidden among the townspeople, attacked the six guards surrounding Little John and knocked them out.

From the windows of nearby houses came more outlaws, swarming down to help Robin who was keeping other guards at bay with his sword. Townsmen and women picked up anything they could lay their hands on to attack and distract the Sheriff's men.

Rallied by another blast from Robin's horn, the outlaws surrounded Little John and began to fight a rearguard action.

With longbows, swords and quarterstaffs, they held off their attackers as they made their way through the streets of Nottingham.

Out through the gates of the town they went and across the bridge that led to the road to Sherwood, closely pressed all the time by the Sheriff's guards.

Once across the bridge, Robin Hood and three of his men stayed back. With their longbows they picked off the pursuing guards one by one, while Little John was able to reach the safety of the forest unharmed.

That night there was a grand celebration under the Greenwood tree!

These were some of the adventures that befell the outlaws, and there were many others in the months that followed. Their fame spread throughout the land. Always it was the same story—take from the rich to give to the poor.

On one occasion, Will Scarlett with Merry Andrew and Much the Miller's son came across a party of three knights with an escort of halberdiers on their way to a jousting tournament.

Merry Andrew shot an arrow that pierced the flag, held on high by the leading knight on his lance, and pinned it to the branch of an oak tree.

Will Scarlett leapt out in front of the astonished group, sword in hand.

"Halt!" he cried. "I have a score of archers in the trees with an arrow aimed at each one of you."

Addressing the leading knight, he said, "A bag of gold pieces is all I ask."

The nearest of the escorts made a movement to bring down his halberd on to Will Scarlett's head. An arrow sped out of the trees and knocked the halberd from his hands.

"The gold!" demanded Will.

Grudgingly, a leather bag was produced and handed over. Not one of them dared make any other movement for fear of an arrow.

"The poor people of Nottingham will bless you," said Will. "Now—be on your way." And he disappeared into the trees.

"They really thought there were twenty of us hidden in the trees!" cried Much— and the three outlaws laughed all the way to the bank where Robin sat under the Greenwood tree.

"Well done, my merry men," he said as they handed over their spoils.

The only thing that Robin Hood would never countenance was any action which might be regarded as disloyal to the King.

Thus, when one of his men, singlehanded, brought in a King's Messenger carrying gold for the Royal Treasury, Robin ordered him him to be freed and sent on his way.

However, anything that might in any way disturb the composure of the Sheriff was fair game.

One day when Little John came back from a visit to Nottingham he immediately won Robin's attention with his news.

"Our friend, the Sheriff," he announced, "is planning to hold an archery contest this coming week."

"Indeed," murmured Robin. "I wonder . . ."

"It seems," went on Little John, "that the noble Lord is worried that his own archers are no match for certain outlaws in Sherwood Forest!"

"Oh-ho!" laughed Robin. "Methinks he worries in good cause!"

"He is offering a silver arrow as the first prize," grinned Little John, "and a year's service in the Sheriff's guard to all the best archers."

Robin rubbed his nose. "I think we might find him a couple of recruits, eh, Little John?"

The archery contest was held on a wide, flat stretch of moorland not far from the town. A large crowd gathered to watch the sport, and there were dozens of competitors with their longbows and quivers full of arrows.

The Sheriff sat in a seat of honour and several of his guards were well in evidence.

Among the competitors, the Sheriff noticed two very dark-skinned men, one of whom wore a beard. He beckoned to one of his guards.

"Find out for me who are these two strangers, and whence they come," he commanded. "We must be on our guard against outlaws."

The guard went across, spoke to the two men and returned to the Sheriff.

"My Lord, the unbearded one says that his name is—er—Nibor, my Lord."

"What name?" asked the Sheriff.

"Er—Nibor, my Lord."

"A strange name," commented the Sheriff.

"He says, my Lord, that he comes from the Orient."

"Ah, that explains it," exclaimed the Sheriff. "And the other?"

"The bearded one, even stranger, my Lord," said the guard. "He calls himself—as I heard it—Elttil Nhoj."

"Also from the Orient," nodded the Sheriff.

"Yes, my Lord."

"Well, let's see how they fare with the longbow." And the Sheriff signalled for the competition to commence.

The target was small and, to start with, it was at 100 paces. Many of the first to shoot missed it altogether; others shot too low and hit the support.

The first to score a bullseye was the bearded stranger.

"Well shot," cried the Sheriff. Well done—er—Elttil—er—well done, my man!"

Next to shoot was the other dark stranger. He quickly took aim and loosed his arrow. There was a gasp from the crowd as it hit the arrow already in the bullseye and split it down the middle.

"Now there's an archer I should welcome in my guard," murmured the Sheriff to himself.

The competition went on all afternoon, but none of the other archers could match the two strangers, so that the result was inevitable.

The Sheriff announced that he would present the silver arrow to the winner, Nibor, who came forward and knelt before him.

Handing over the prize, the Sheriff said, "You shoot a goodly arrow my man, though you come from afar and boast a strange name."

"Nibor, my Lord. In full, Nibor Dooh."

"Very strange," said the Sheriff.

"Sire, I come from a backward country."

There was a sound that might have been a strangled laugh from the bearded stranger.

"I wish you well in Nottingham," added the Sheriff.

The two strangers left the field together. As soon as they were out of earshot, the one called Nibor said, "Little John, you nearly gave the game away!"

"Oh, Robin! Nibor Dooh—from a backward country!" And Little John roared with laughter.

"Well, it's not as bad as Elttil Nhoj," said Robin. "Anyway, I have no use for this silver arrow. I've a mind to send it back where it came from."

"With a little message for his Lordship?"

"That's a good idea, Little John!"

So it happened that when the Sheriff of Nottingham was enjoying his supper that evening, there was the swish of an arrow coming through the window. It thumped on to the table. It was a silver arrow that he recognized immediately, and attached to it was a message:

"With the compliments of Robin Hood
and his backward friend Nibor Dooh"

In his anger, the Sheriff swept the rest of his supper from the table and swore vengeance—once again—on Robin Hood.

By this time, Robin Hood and the outlaws were so well-established in Sherwood Forest that he felt it was safe to send for his sweetheart, Marian.

A marriage was arranged. Friar Tuck conducted the wedding ceremony and Little John acted as best man.

All the outlaws were there to wish the couple every happiness and a great feast was planned for the evening.

But, unbeknown to Robin, the Sheriff had heard the news of the marriage from a tinker who had been passing through the forest and had witnessed the preparations.

The Sheriff at once mustered as many men as he could and led them into the forest, guided by the tinker.

From several directions the Sheriff's men burst into the clearing. The outlaws grabbed their longbows, swords and quarterstaffs to defend themselves.

Robin and the outlaws were, for once, completely relaxed and looking forward to a party when they heard the Sheriff's voice from the trees.

"ATTACK!" he roared.

Robin shouted to two of his men, "Guard Marian with your lives!" Then he entered the fray with the rest of them.

The battle raged for several minutes. The outlaws fought like men possessed, but all too soon the tactics of the Sheriff's guards became evident.

They were after Robin Hood himself!

Soon they had him separated from the rest of
his men. It took four, five, six men to hold him
down, while the rest of the guards kept the
outlaws, desperately trying to rescue their leader,
at bay.

At last, Robin was completely overpowered by sheer weight of numbers, while the wildly excited Sheriff, on horseback in the background, cried, "Bind him, men! Bind him and put a noose around his neck! If he escapes this time, I'll hang the lot of you!"

As evening fell over the forest, a sad sight was seen by the few who witnessed it.

Robin Hood, the bold leader of the outlaws, hands tied tightly behind his back, was being led by a halter round his neck to Nottingham and certain execution.

But they had a long way to go—and it was getting dark.

Fearing an attack by the outlaws, the Sheriff ordered his men to find a suitable place to keep their captive overnight.

They found an old woman living alone in an isolated cottage.

"Put him in there," ordered the Sheriff, "and post plenty of guards. Let him have an old witch for company."

So Robin was bundled into the one room of the cottage. The old woman recognized him. As soon as the door was shut and guarded outside, she whispered: "Master Robin! I am old and bent—if only I had sufficient strength in these old bones to help you . . . !"

Robin whispered in reply, "Mother! Perhaps you can . . . !"

Next morning at daybreak armed guards opened the door of the cottage.

"Come on, out of there, Mister Robin Hood!"

The stooped figure in Lincoln green, hands tied behind the back, limped to the door and went outside with the guards; the noose was put in place and off they went.

A few seconds later, a figure in the old woman's clothes sprinted out of the cottage and was lost in the forest before anyone could stop him. Robin had outwitted the Sheriff again!

The first job Robin and his men had to do was to find a new site for a camp. They soon found a suitable spot and Robin was reunited with his bride of a few days.

It was Marian who told him of the news from London—King Richard was now in England, back from his latest crusade.

"I wonder if we'll get a chance to see him," pondered Robin.

That chance came sooner than expected.

The King had heard from his nobles that there were outlaws in a certain Sherwood Forest, near Nottingham, who were making free with the Royal herds of deer. Indeed, it was said that on several occasions they had even given away venison to the poor people in the surrounding districts!

The King was angry.

"Who has charge of my herds up there?" he demanded.

"The Sheriff of Nottingham, Sire," he was told.

"Methinks I must ride north to Nottingham and beyond to inspect my estates," said the King.

And so it was arranged.

The journey north took many days. The King was escorted by a party of knights and nobles and everywhere they stopped they heard nothing but good about the outlaws in Sherwood and little but bad about the Sheriff of Nottingham.

The King became more and more impressed.

"It would seem," he said, discussing it with his advisers, "that this outlaw, Robin Hood, takes only from rich men, and not for his own profit, but to give to the poor and deserving. A worthy cause, indeed!"

"But he also takes what he wants from your herds, Sire," pointed out one of the nobles.

"Ah, yes—my deer," agreed the King. "We shall see."

As they approached Sherwood, the King was advised to disguise himself as an abbott in case of attack. Once in the forest, sure enough, three men in Lincoln green leapt out of the trees to confront them.

"What's this?" demanded the King.

"Have no fear, Sir Abbott," said Robin Hood, "We are simply asking you to sup with us."

"You take not my money?"

"If you have some to spare, sir, we might ask you to pay for your dinner," smiled Robin.

"So that's the way of it," laughed the King, dismounting. "You're a man after my own heart, Robin Hood!"

"And you're no abbott, I'll warrant!"

"I am your King!" and he opened his robes to reveal the Royal Arms on his breastplate.

The three archers went on their knees before him.

"Welcome to the Greenwood, Sire," said Robin.

The King eyed him sternly. "They tell me that you and your rogues have been making free of my herds!"

"Sire, we have been but culling them to keep their numbers down. There be as many head of deer in the forest today as when your majesty left."

"If that be so, Robin Hood, you have our royal pardon," The King turned to two of his knights. "Go and find that wretched Sheriff and take him away to await my pleasure."

"So now, Robin Hood," he added, "a moment hence you offered us a dinner!"

"Sire," answered Robin, "A right royal feast it shall be!"

Pardoned by the King, and loved by all except the few rich people he had relieved of some of their wealth, Robin Hood continued to live in Sherwood Forest.

He could never bear to leave the Greenwood.

The outlaws were disbanded. Most of them returned to their homes—which some had not seen for many a year.

But a few of his closest companions chose to stay with Robin in the forest; Little John, of course, and Friar Tuck amongst them. And Marian was there, too, to look after them all.

It is said that when Robin Hood was very old, with barely enough strength left to handle his longbow, he shot his last arrow into the forest.

"Wherever that arrow falls," he said to his friends, "there shall be my grave."

And so it was.

THE END

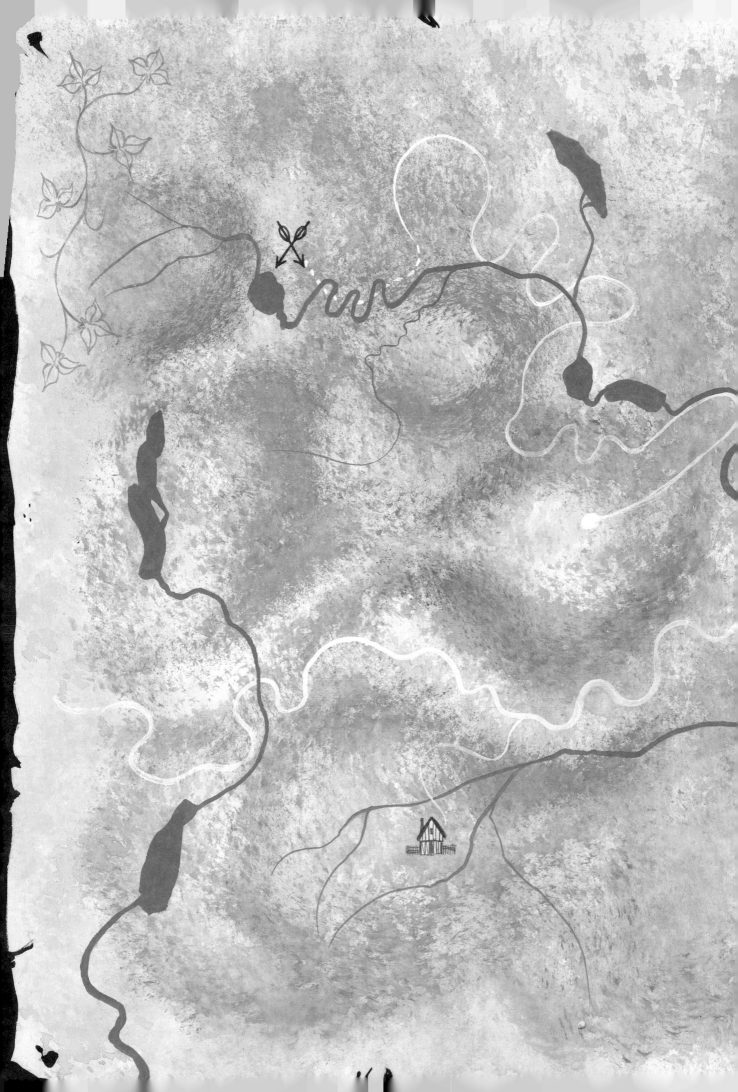